White Rabbit's Color Book

Alan Baker

KINGFISHER

NEW YORK

KINGFISHER
LONDON & NEW YORK

Copyright © Alan Baker 1994

Published in the United States by Kingfisher,
175 Fifth Avenue, New York, NY 10010
Kingfisher is an imprint of Macmillan Children's Books, London.
All rights reserved.

Distributed in the U.S. by Macmillan,
175 Fifth Avenue, New York, NY 10010
Distributed in Canada by H.B. Fenn and Company Ltd.,
34 Nixon Road, Bolton, Ontario L7E 1W2

LIBRARY OF CONGRESS CATALOGING-IN-PUBLICATION DATA
Baker, Alan.
White Rabbit's Color Book/Alan Baker.
—1st American ed.
p.   cm. — (Little rabbit books)
Summary: White Rabbit hops from one paint pot to
another, changing colors as he goes, until he ends up brown.
[1. Color—Fiction. 2. Rabbits—Fiction.]
I. Title. II. Series: Baker, Alan. Little rabbit books.
PZ7.B1688Wj   1994
[E]—dc20   93-32316   CIP AC

ISBN 978-0-7534-5254-7

Printed in Singapore

16 18 20 19 17

For more information, please visit
www.kingfisherbooks.com

One day, White Rabbit found
three big tubs of paint,
red, yellow, and blue.

Sunshine yellow,
she thought.
Lovely.

A quick dip
and ...

... yellow rabbit,
bright as the Sun.

Now what about red,
thought Rabbit.

What's this?
Orange Rabbit?
Look. Red and yellow
together make
orange!

Time for
a wash,
thought
Rabbit.

Red on its own this time.

Splash!

Red Rabbit,
sizzling hot red.

How cool blue looks, thought Rabbit.

What's this? Purple Rabbit? Look. Red and blue together make purple. I'm a very important Royal Purple Rabbit.

Princess
Purple
Rabbit
in the shower.

Blue will do,
thought Rabbit.

Blue Rabbit,
icy cold blue.
Brrr.

How warm
yellow looks,
thought Rabbit.

What's this?
Green Rabbit.
Look. Blue
and yellow
together make
green!

Oh dear,
no more
water.

All that's left is
a little red paint.

Now what would happen? thought Rabbit.

Hooray! Brown Rabbit. Lovely warm brown. Blue, yellow, and red together make brown. And brown's just right for me.